First published in English copyright © 1998 Abbeville Press.
First published in French copyright © 1997 Editions Nathan, Paris. All rights reserved
under international copyright conventions. No part of this book may be reproduced or
utilized in any form or by any means, electronic or mechanical, including photocopying,
recording, or by any information storage and retrieval system, without permission in
writing from the publisher. Inquiries should be addressed to Abbeville Publishing Group,
22 Cortlandt Street, New York, NY 10007. The text of this book was set in Journal Text.
Printed and bound in France.

First edition
2 4 6 8 10 9 7 5 3 1

Library of Congress Cataloging-in-Publication Data
Little Red Riding Hood : a Grimm fairy tale / illustrated by Jean-François Martin.
p. cm. — (The little pebbles)
Summary: A little girl meets a hungry wolf in the forest while on her way
to visit her sick grandmother.
ISBN 0-7892-0421-5
[1. Fairy tales. 2. Folklore—Germany.] I. Martin, Jean-François, 1967– ill.
II. Rothkäppchen. English. III. Little Red Riding Hood. English. IV. Series.
PZ8.L733 1998
398.2'0943'02—dc21   97-23045

Little Red Riding Hood

A Fairy Tale by Grimm
Illustrated by Jean-François Martin

The
Little Pebbles
· Abbeville Kids ·
A Division of Abbeville Publishing Group
New York · London · Paris

Once upon a time there was a little girl who everyone loved from the moment they met her. Her grandmother, who loved her more than anyone, gave her a beautiful riding hood of red velvet. The little girl liked it so much that she wore it all the time, and so everyone called her Little Red Riding Hood.

One day her mother said to her, "Little Red Riding Hood, here's a piece of pie and a bottle of wine. Please take them to your poor sick grandmother. She needs a treat! Now, leave right away before it gets too hot. Don't run off the path, or you might break the bottle of wine. And don't forget to say, 'Hello, how are you?' when you walk in."

"Don't worry, I'll do as you say," promised Little Red Riding Hood, and she waved and set off.

Little Red Riding Hood's grandmother lived a good half-hour from town, in the woods over the hills. And as soon as the little girl entered the forest, she met a wolf. She didn't know how sneaky this particular animal can be, so she wasn't at all afraid.

"Hello, Little Red Riding Hood," said the wolf.

"Hello, wolf."

"Where are you off to this fine morning?"

"To visit my grandma. She's sick. I'm bringing her a piece of pie and some wine."

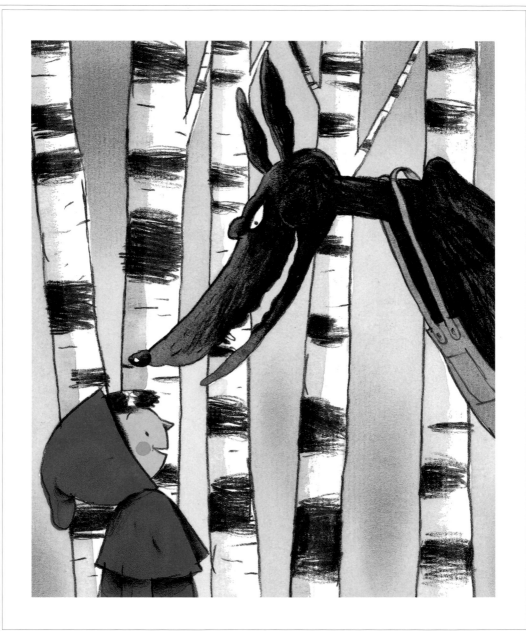

"And where does your grandmother live, Little Red Riding Hood?" asked the wolf.

"Her house is through the woods, under three big oak trees, a little ways from here."

As he walked along the path with her, the wolf was thinking to himself: "What a delightful little girl. Plump and tender—just right! She'll certainly be tastier than the grandmother. Yes, much tastier! I must make a plan so I can eat them both."

"What's this?" the wolf said, stopping suddenly. "Look at all the beautiful wildflowers growing here in the woods. And listen to the sweet song of the birds! The forest is such a cheerful place— you should stay and enjoy it for a little while."

Little Red Riding Hood looked, and saw the beautiful rays of the sun dancing among the trees and colorful flowers everywhere. "If I bring a bunch of flowers to Grandma," she thought to herself, "they'll make her happy. It's still early. I have time to pick them."

Little Red Riding Hood left the path to look for flowers: one over here, another one over there, and always the prettiest flower was just a little farther away and a little deeper in the woods.

Meanwhile, the wolf ran ahead to the grandmother's house and knocked on her door.

"It's Little Red Riding Hood," called the wolf,
"and I've brought you a piece of pie and some
wine. Open the door!"

"Pull the latch and the door will open!"

So the wolf pulled down the latch, pushed open
the door, ran to the grandmother's bed, and ate
her! Then he put on her nightgown, covered his
head with her lace bonnet, closed the curtains,
and climbed into bed.

By now Little Red Riding Hood had picked so
many flowers that she could hardly carry them
all. She found her way back to the path and
headed for her grandmother's house. When she
got there, she found the door already open.

When Little Red Riding Hood entered the
bedroom, she had a feeling that something
wasn't right.

When she said hello, no one answered, and so
she opened the bed curtains. Grandma was there
in bed with her bonnet hiding almost all of her
face. She seemed different somehow. . . .

"Why Grandma, what big ears you have!"

"The better to hear you with, my child."

"Why Grandma, what big eyes you have!"

"The better to see you with, my sweet."

"Why Grandma, what big hands you have!"

"The better to hold you with, my dear."

"Why Grandma, what big teeth you have!"

"The better to eat you with!" growled the wolf as he jumped out of bed and gobbled up poor Little Red Riding Hood.

Full and satisfied, the wolf fell asleep on the bed. But he snored so loudly that a passing hunter heard him.

"Now why is the old lady snoring so loudly?" the hunter wondered. "I'll go and see if she's alright."

The hunter entered the house and found the wolf there sleeping in the bed.

"So it's you, you scoundrel!" said the hunter, and he lifted his rifle.

He was about to shoot when he realized that the wolf might have eaten the old lady and that he might be able to rescue her. So he put down his gun and started to cut open the belly of the wolf with some scissors.

After the second or third cut, the hunter saw a little red velvet hood; after a few more cuts, the little girl leaped out. "I was so afraid in there! It was so dark!"

A little while later, out came the grandmother as well.

The wolf, of course, did not survive this operation, and so that was the end of him. The hunter took the wolf's fur to sell and gave some of it to Little Red Riding Hood, so that her mother could make her a nice fur coat. Everyone was happy. Grandma enjoyed the piece of pie and wine. And Little Red Riding Hood was especially glad just to be safe. She had been so scared that she promised to be more careful and always stay on the path.

Look carefully at these pictures from the story.
They're all mixed up. Can you put them back
in the right order?

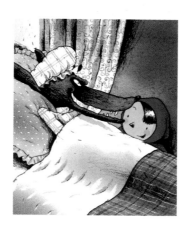